Gift of Years

by
Lucy Woodward and Margaret Wyatt

ARK BOOKS
Minneapolis, MN 55401
(a subsidiary of MIDWEST CHALLENGE, INC.)

Cover Art:
ART GORE

Gift of Years

Thought Treasures for Those Growing Older

by
Lucy Woodward and Margaret Wyatt

Gift of Years

Table of Contents

Scripture references taken from NEB are so indicated and are used by permission. Those marked NAS are from the New American Standard Bible, © the Lockman Foundation 1960, 1962, 1963, 1968, 1971, 1972, 1973, 1975.

About the Cover

"Cattails," our cover art for this collection, is taken from the renowned works of artist-photographer Art Gore, whose studio and gallery are located in Morrison, Colorado.

Mr. Gore, whose magnificent still-lifes "speak softly to the echoes"* of the past, is indeed a preserver of yesterdays—a master scenographer who captures the beauty of antiquity and gives the viewer a glimpse into the eternal truth of existence.

"Cattails" whispers a breathtaking message to the heart and expresses, with soul-precision, exactly what it is this book is all about.

*SPEAK SOFTLY TO THE ECHOES, a collection of still-lifes and prose by Art Gore, Northland Press, Flagstaff, Arizona, 1978.

A Note from the Publisher

Whether you are sixteen or ninety-six, here is a book that will make your heart sing. Though written as God's gift to those who are growing older, the selections contained herein address all human emotions and conditions, whether they be expressed in joy, sorrow, fear, pain, loneliness, regret or change.

With a depth that belies their years, the writers of these inspired poems and meditations have succeeded in lifting mankind's most poignant concerns into the light of God's presence, thus giving an illumined perspective which speaks of glorious promise.

From the tranquil, rich prose of Margaret Wyatt to the tender, exquisite poetry of Lucy Woodward, to the soul-stirring scripture quoted from God's Holy Word, you will find a blessing on every page and a hope that will enrich your being throughout the years to come.

The Publisher

A Note from the Authors

This collection of poems and meditations came into being as the result of a need. As a volunteer worker in a Christian ministry which calls on the aged and shut-ins in Casper, Wyoming, Margaret was searching for appropriate printed material to leave with those she was visiting. There was none available. Even the quarterly devotional she had been using stopped coming. She began to pray about it.

God's answer came on three consecutive days. On the first, the message was clear and simple: "Write one." On the second, a further directive was given: "Ask Lucy Woodward to work on it with you." On the third, at a prayer meeting, we both felt led to be His instruments in this project.

That night each of us was inspired to write seven devotions. On a second occasion, each of us wrote three; and on a third occasion, each of us wrote again seven. We were working independently at all times and had no idea the other was receiving simultaneously.

Knowing that the numbers *three* and *seven* have special significance in God's kingdom, we were thrilled to notice His use of that pattern in leading us. Our guidance was identical in that each selection was written as though God is speaking directly to the older person.

It is our prayer that all who read these meditations will find lasting messages of hope, peace and joy and be drawn closer to Him.

LW and MW

Frontispiece

*"You who have been borne by Me from
    birth,
And have been carried from the womb;
Even to your old age, I shall be the same,
And even to your graying years I shall
    bear you!
I have done it, and I shall carry you;
And I shall bear you, and I shall deliver
    you."*

                  Isaiah 46:3-4 (NAS)

Gift of Beauty

Who is a wise man and endued with knowledge among you? Let him show out of a good conversation his works with meekness of wisdom.

James 3:13

. . . that their hearts may be encouraged . . . and attaining to all the wealth that comes from the full assurance of understanding, resulting in a true knowledge of God's mystery, that is, Christ Himself, in whom are hidden all the treasures of wisdom and knowledge.

Colossians 2:2-3 (NAS)

ALSO
Psalm 51:6

THE FRUITFUL YEARS

What wisdom and beauty I see in you! There is a depth the young do not possess. What precious words come from your lips! They have been born of the learning times of life—the times you have spent with Me.

As you share the lessons you have learned, others will know that our spirits have been joined, and that you speak an overflowing of the very words I would give to them.

Use these gifts to bless the young, the seeking, the lost. Touch them with the tenderness the years have given to you. Such seeming quiet task has great significance; for I would have you know these are the fruitful years.

Wisdom is with aged men, with long life is understanding.

Job 12:12 (NAS)

But solid food is for the mature, who because of practice have their senses trained to discern good and evil. Therefore leaving the elementary teaching about the Christ, let us press on to maturity . . .

Hebrews 5:14, 6:1a (NAS)

ALSO

I Corinthians 2:6-7, 10
II Corinthians 10:5

YOUR RIPENED DAYS

I bless you in these, your ripened days,
*   For I can see the many ways in which*
You've learned to live in fullest flower.
*   The richness of your harvest field*
Is ample witness of a lifetime
*   Yielded to My Spirit's Power.*

At this, your autumn hour,
*   You've grown beyond illusion,*
Known security in age and knowing Me,
*   And in maturing*
*   Found new purity.*

No confusion blocks the stream
*   Where My clean Love can flow;*
No conflict rages deep within your shining soul,
*   That has one simple goal,*
*   To live for Me.*

And he fell to the earth, and heard a voice saying unto him, Saul, Saul, why persecutest thou me? And he said, Who art thou, Lord? And the Lord said, I am Jesus whom thou persecutest: it is hard for thee to kick against the pricks.

Acts 9:4-5

ALSO
Mark 9:23-24
John 20:25-28

CONQUEST

I love the way you've let the years
    Shape and soften your face
With light of laughter and shadow of tears
    And acceptance of My Grace.

It took a long time—you were once so wild!
    So tortured by unrest—
The ones who struggled to become My child
    Passed the hardest test!

And God said, Let there be light: and there was light. And God saw the light, that it was good: and God divided the light from the darkness. And God called the light Day . . . and the evening and the morning were the first day.

Genesis 1:3-5

This is the day which the Lord hath made; we will rejoice and be glad in it.

Psalm 118:24

SUNRISE PORTRAIT

With silver and rose I paint My skies:
*   A greeting card for you,*
Catching the color of your eyes
*   With just a trace of blue;*

Brushing the ever-shifting space
*   With irridescent hue,*
Matching the blush of your sleeping face
*   To dawn's rays peeking through . . .*

Good morning, My love, it's another bright day;
*   Everything in it is new!*
With this little card I just wanted to say
*   How much I'll always love you!*

A gray head is a crown of glory; It is found in the way of righteousness.

Proverbs 16:31 (NAS)

For Thou didst form my inward parts; Thou didst weave me in my mother's womb. I will give thanks to Thee, for I am fearfully and wonderfully made; Wonderful are Thy works, and my soul knows it very well.

Psalm 139:13-14 (NAS)

ALSO
Philippians 1:6
Isaiah 49:5

BEAUTY OF YEARS

The silver in your hair is a precious crown and glorious to behold. You have beauty that comes with the years—a radiance that only time can bestow. Your searching has been stilled and now you reap the harvest of joy in Me. I knew you in your mother's womb; and when I see the gift of your life which you have given back to Me, I cannot but say, "It is good."

For thou, O God, hast proved us: thou hast tried us, as silver is tried.

Psalm 66:10

Thou art all fair, my love; there is no spot in thee.

Song of Solomon 4:7

MY TREASURE

You are of so much worth to Me; you are My treasure. My Soul is so tender toward you.

You have been refined and are like the purest gold—more precious you are than perfect rubies.

Your eyes are like eternal stars and how they twinkle though they may have grown dim with years. I see for you and I see such beauty, for you are My delight.

I rejoice in you.

Every good gift and every perfect gift is from above, and cometh down from the Father of lights, with whom is no variableness, neither shadow of turning.

James 1:17

For the mountains shall depart, and the hills be removed; but my kindness shall not depart from thee, neither shall the covenant of my peace be removed, saith the Lord that hath mercy on thee.

Isaiah 54:10

ALSO

Romans 8:28
Isaiah 55:8

KALEIDOSCOPE

People change, Beloved, with the passing of
    time.
There is change in growth, and growth in
    accepting the change in those you love.
Perhaps you too are different now.

My world is a kaleidoscope of shifting colors
    in ordered patterns.
One turn, and all is new.
    Never twice the same design, but always
        in perfect symmetry.

Has something shifted, changing the pattern of
    your life?
    Are the colors different now?
Are you surprised or saddened by the people you
    love?
    Did you expect more of them than they could
        give?
It's part of My ordered pattern for your life.
Accept it and grow, My child, and live.

. . . speaking to one another in psalms and hymns and spiritual songs, singing and making melody with your heart to the Lord . . .
Ephesians 5:19 (NAS)

For many are called, but few are chosen.
Matthew 22:14

ALSO
John 13:34

MY MELODY

There's a song in the hearts of My older friends
    That cannot be heard in the young,
A song of beginnings and middles and ends,
    And I love to hear it sung!

It's a delicate melody rippling along;
    It's a tune that touches My Heart,
For it's played upon strings that are supple and
    strong,
    That never can be worn apart!

The way that you live is the melody;
    You're one of My chosen few:
Your life is in perfect harmony
    For you've loved as I've loved you.

Gift of Memories

I wish you all joy in the Lord. I will say it again: all joy be yours. Let your magnanimity be manifest to all. The Lord is near; have no anxiety, but in everything make your requests known to God in prayer and petition with thanksgiving. Then the peace of God, which is beyond our utmost understanding, will keep guard over your hearts and your thoughts, in Christ Jesus. And now, my friends, all that is true, all that is noble, all that is just and pure, all that is lovable and gracious, whatever is excellent and admirable—fill all your thoughts with these things.

Philippians 4:4-8 (NEB)

ALSO

Proverbs 8:30-31
Isaiah 65:19

EARLY MEMORIES

Do you sometimes wonder why
  I quicken memories of early years
And bring them brightly to the forefront of your
      mind,
  And at the same time you forget
Who came to see you just an hour ago?
  Don't fret, My dear, I only want
These later days for you to be
  Brimming full of happy memory!

Time is not a problem in My world;
  Past joys are just as real today.
You're just as loved right now as when I first
  Conceived the thought of you
Before the world began.

And now I'm preparing your pliant mind
  To compass only joy.
All sorrow will soon be left behind,
  Its purpose done.

You're My beloved just as you are;
  Now rest, and live again in early joys,
And let Me joy with you!

And they brought young children to him, that he should touch them: and his disciples rebuked those that brought them. But when Jesus saw it, he was much displeased, and said unto them, Suffer the little children to come unto me, and forbid them not: for of such is the kingdom of God. Verily I say unto you, Whosoever shall not receive the kingdom of God as a little child, he shall not enter therein. And he took them up in his arms, put his hands upon them, and blessed them.

Mark 10:13-16

ALSO
Ezekiel 34:16
Psalm 149:1-5

AS A LITTLE CHILD

Are you grown up enough to be a child?
You know I said you must
   approach Me as a little one
     in perfect trust.
     It's hard to do.

Especially when you're four-score years or
   more—
To disentangle from the fears
   brought on by all that went before
   to hurt and to dishearten you.

But children forget, and so must you.
Give it all to Me.
   Laugh and sing!
   And let Me make you new!

Ye are my friends, if ye do whatsoever I command you. Henceforth I call you not servants; for the servant knoweth not what his lord doeth: but I have called you friends; for all things that I have heard of my father I have made known unto you.

John 15:14-15

ALSO

Isaiah 30:15
Proverbs 3:5-6

TIME FOR ME

Remember the time when you were young
    And always in a hurry?
Your mind in such a frantic flurry,
    So filled with thoughts of things to do
You never heard what I said to you?

Now at last there's time for Me,
    And oh, how I rejoice!
Because you're listening to My Voice,
    And sharing with Me each precious plan,
As one can do with a trusted Friend!

And I will give unto thee the keys of the kingdom of heaven: and whatsoever thou shalt bind on earth shall be bound in heaven: and whatsoever thou shalt loose on earth shall be loosed in heaven.

Matthew 16:19

In the fear of the Lord is strong confidence: and his children shall have a place of refuge.
Proverbs 14:26

ALSO
John 1:11-13

MY PLAN FOR YOU

Do you sometimes look back over your life and remember times of joy— times of happiness? Thank Me for them. If times of sorrow come to mind, thank Me for these too, for these were the times I was drawing you closer to Me. It was during the valleys you reached for My Hand, and I was able to come to you and shower My love down on you. It was all a part of My plan for you.

Therefore if thou bring thy gift to the altar, and there rememberest that thy brother hath ought against thee; leave there thy gift before the altar, and go thy way; first be reconciled to thy brother, and then come and offer thy gift.

Matthew 5:23-24

Create in me a clean heart, O God; and renew a right spirit within me.

Psalm 51:10

ALSO
Matthew 18:21-22

FORGIVENES

My precious child,
    Is there someone still remaining
        memory
Through the long corridors of the years
    Whom you have not forgiven?

Do it now!

Have you been driven to a bitterness
    So great it overwhelms you?

Let Me help!

I can clear it all away and make you well;
    I will help you to forgive—just ask Me to!
Just say you want to do it; just begin:
    "Lord, help me, please!"
Behold, the thing is done; I see no sin!
    Clean you are, and well again!

It is the Lord who directs a man's steps, he holds him firm and watches over his path. Though he may fall, he will not go headlong, for the Lord grasps him by the hand. I have been young and am now grown old, and never have I seen a righteous man forsaken.

Psalm 37:23-35 (NEB)

ALSO

Psalm 25:4-5

WALKING WITH M

As you look back over the
the valleys, do not fret over the things
that might have been, because you have
been walking with Me; and the path I
marked out for you, you have followed.

I have seen the times you stumbled,
but I have seen the times you got back
up and started again, trusting though
you knew not where the path would
lead. Your faith has been a joy to Me,
and many are your rewards in heaven.

Gift of Assurance

I can do all things through Christ which strengtheneth me.

Philippians 4:13

My grace is sufficient for thee: for my strength is made perfect in weakness.

II Corinthians 12:9

ALSO

Matthew 26:40
Isaiah 49:5

MY STRENGTH

Beloved, are you tired today?

Remember, there were times when I was tired too—times when I was lonely.

It was those times that I reached up to the Father and drew My strength from Him, as you must draw from Me.

My strength will flow into you, all you have need of for this day.

They arrived at Bethsaida. There the people brought a blind man to Jesus and begged him to touch him. He took the blind man by the hand and led him away out of the village. Then he spat on his eyes, laid his hands upon him, and asked whether he could see anything. The man's sight began to come back, and he said, "I see men; they look like trees, but they are walking about." Jesus laid his hands on his eyes again; he looked hard, and now he was cured so that he saw everything clearly.

Mark 8:22-26 (NEB)

ALSO
Psalm 19:8

EYES

Is it difficult to read this print?
    Do you want a second touch?
Or, Beloved, is it better in your wisdom
    to shut your eyes and let the inner pictures
        play?
Sometimes I give the blind a kind of vision
    that the sighted cannot grasp.
(Men see best when least distracted
    by the things they see.)
The paintbrush of imagination wielded by the
    Master's hand can brighten all your dreams.
So let Me touch those dimming eyes with gentle
        balm;
    shut them now and see Reality.

Thou wilt keep him in perfect peace, whose mind is stayed on thee: because he trusteth in thee.

Isaiah 26:3

Acquaint now thyself with him, and be at peace: thereby good shall come unto thee.

Job 22:21

ALSO

John 15:4

ABIDE IN ME

Today I wish to bring you peace. As you are relaxing, lift up your soul, your spirit, your mind to Me and absorb My peace. Picture Me looking down on you—My hands stretched out to you—My peace and love flowing out to you. Can you not feel My presence? Does your spirit quicken with My love? Each time you seek Me, you will feel Me close to you, for I am with you always. Abide in Me, for I abide in you.

Who shall separate us from the love of Christ? Shall tribulation, or distress, or persecution, or famine, or nakedness, or peril, or sword? As it is written, for thy sake we are killed all the day long; we are accounted as sheep for the slaughter. Nay, in all these things we are more than conquerors through him that loved us. For I am persuaded, that neither death, nor life, nor angels, nor principalities, nor powers, nor things present, nor things to come, nor height, nor depth, nor any other creature, shall be able to separate us from the love of God, which is in Christ Jesus our Lord.

Romans 8:35-39

ALSO
John 17:21-22

54

I WILL NEVER LEAVE YO

Do you feel alone today?
　　But I am here!
There is no wall between;
　　No barrier of age or pain
Can separate, but rather makes us one.
　　I know all hurt; no passing time
Can mute your pleading call to Me.
　　I hear it instantly and am within,
Easing, soothing, sharing
　　Your joy and pain.
I see My weeping eyes in yours;
　　My suffering and My love
Still softening and deepening your face until
　　Another looking thus into your eyes
Sees joy, and peace, and grace—sees Me.

from Ashley
to
one!

Turn to me and be gracious to me, for I am lonely and afflicted. The troubles of my heart are enlarged; bring me out of my distresses.
                                  Psalm 25-16-17 (NAS)

And God shall wipe away all tears from their eyes; and there shall be no more death, neither sorrow, nor crying, neither shall there be any more pain: for the former things are passed away.
                                  Revelation 21:4

ALSO
I John 4:18
II Timothy 1:7

CALL AND I WILL COM

I heard you calling in the night
    From your lonely sleep,
And instantly I came to you
    And told you not to weep.

I came and sat here for a while
    To quiet any fear,
And then in sleep you slowly smiled,
    Knowing I was here.

Amen!

If we believe not, yet he abideth faithful: he cannot deny himself.

II Timothy 2:13

The eternal God is thy refuge, and underneath are the everlasting arms. . .

Deuteronomy 33:27

ALSO

Matthew 6:33-34
Colossians 2:13-14

MY EVERLASTING ARMS

There are no limits to My love,
   No way I can withhold it
      nor deny thy need
Lest I deny My own Identity.

But blessings are bestowed on thee
   Like fine, gray summer rain,
      And thou art freed
From all thy tangled web
   Of vain anxiety
Knit randomly through cold and painful years
   Of fleeing Me.

Don't weep, 'tis done! Behold,
   The knotted past is cut away!
And naught remains but one bright Thread
   Still holding thee tight to Me!
And underneath,
   My everlasting arms upholding thee!

That which we have seen and heard declare we unto you, that ye also may have fellowship with us: and truly our fellowship is with the Father, and with his Son, Jesus Christ.

I John 1:3

My voice shalt thou hear in the morning, O Lord; in the morning will I direct my prayer unto thee, and will look up.

Psalm 5:3

ALSO
Exodus 15:2

TAKE ME WITH YOU

Lift up your eyes and your heart to Me, and I will come to you. I wish to visit you and be part of your day. As you go about your daily tasks, take Me with you. Such joy and fellowship we shall have together! With your hand in mine, My strength becomes your strength. All is well, dear one. Look unto Me.

Scripture says, "I will destroy the wisdom of the wise, and bring to nothing the cleverness of the clever." Where is your wise man now, your man of learning, or your subtle debater—limited, all of them, to this passing age? God has made the wisdom of this world look foolish.

I Corinthians 1:19-21 (NEB)

ALSO

II Corinthians 5:17
Ephesians 4:23-24

WISDOM

What's that? You've had such a rude surprise?
  You thought that when you grew this old
And learned this much,
  You'd have all the treasures of the wise?
And they'd suffice?

But now you're bored and dull,
  And thoughts revolve around themselves
In endlessness without a goal.
  All conversations rot because the people talk
Of things that you once learned and then forgot,
  And now no longer care to know.

My dear, perhaps that's true,
  But think on this:
Behold, in Me all things are new!

That tulip, this child's smile, a moment's
  Sun-filled joy, serenity . . .
The most precious wisdom you could have
  Is knowing Me.

But seek ye first the kingdom of God, and his righteousness; and all these things shall be added unto you.

Matthew 6:33

And I say unto you, Ask, and it shall be given you; seek, and ye shall find; knock, and it shall be opened unto you. For every one that asketh receiveth; and he that seeketh findeth; and to him that knocketh it shall be opened. If a son shall ask bread of any of you that is a father, will he give him a stone? or if he ask a fish, will he for a fish give him a serpent? Or if he shall ask an egg, will he offer him a scorpion? If ye, then, being evil, know how to give good gifts unto your children: how much more shall your heavenly Father give the Holy Spirit to them that ask him?

Luke 11:9-13

TREASURE THESE THI

You are my child, no matter the number of your years. I delight in supplying your needs, and I know them before you are ever aware of them.

I prepare special surprises for you, just to see the joy on your face!

Treasure these things, for they are a part of Me.

Gift of Usefulness

... but you shall receive power when the Holy Spirit has come upon you; and you shall be My witnesses both in Jerusalem, and in all Judea and Samaria, and even to the remotest part of the earth.

Acts 1:8

ALSO
I Corinthians 2:9a, 10-11a
Psalm 119:105

FOLLOW MY SPIRIT

Did you hear a whispering
   Just the other day
Insisting that you get up and do
   Before the urge went away?

That was My Spirit telling you
   That inside you're strong and young,
And it's high time for you to do something new!
   There's another new song to be sung!

There's another new friend to make today
   Who needs all the love you can give,
So follow my calling, go all of the way;
   You'll get younger the longer you live!

Commit to the Lord all that you do, and your plans will be fulfilled.

Proverbs 16:3 (NEB)

And whatsoever ye do in word or deed, do all in the name of the Lord Jesus, giving thanks to God and the Father by him.

Colossians 3:17

And the King shall answer and say unto them, Verily I say unto you, Inasmuch as ye have done it unto one of the least of these my brethren, ye have done it unto me.

Matthew 25:40

REACHING OUT IN LOVE

Beloved, put your heart into doing something for Me today! Write a letter, paint a picture, bake a cake—just something to express your love. How pleased I will be when you make that effort! I'll be blessed and you will gladden someone's heart!

Behold, I stand at the door, and knock: if any man hear my voice, and open the door, I will come in to him, and will sup with him, and he with me.

Revelation 3:20

And therefore will the Lord wait, that he may be gracious unto you . . .

Isaiah 30:18

WILL YOU WAIT WITH ME?

There are some who don't believe in Me;
   I ache for them, and, grieving,
      Long to force the gate—
      The secret sanctuary of their souls
      Where even I can't enter in, unbidden.

So I wait outside and try
   To draw their hidden spirits nigh unto My
      own,
A lonely vigil:
   Will you wait with Me?

Their empty lives—in darkness spent,
   Unceasing motion bent on tinseled
      happiness—
      Poor substitute for peace.
How could I cease my prayers for these,
   The lost, who never knew the Fold
   Or heard their Shepherd's call?

Wait awhile with Me, I pray;
   A word, a touch, a smile from you
Might be the very way
   To open up these darkened hearts
      And let our Love shine through.

But thou art holy, O thou that inhabitest the praises of Israel.

Psalm 22:3

Verily, verily, I say unto you, He that believeth on me, the works that I do shall he do also; and greater works than these shall he do; because I go unto My Father.

John 14:12

ALSO

I Corinthians 2:16
John 7:38

I INHABIT YOUR PRAISES

Did you know that your spirit blesses Me?
   You give Me joy and I live in your silent
      songs of praise!
The music in your heart bathes and renews Me.
   You are a fine-tuned instrument
Perfected with practice and tears and age;
   Mellowed with years, smooth, and making
Perfect inner harmony.

You are one of my precious few, a chosen one.
   You think, "But Lord, it can't be true!
I cannot speak or move!"
   Be still and know
   That there's a river of love flowing
Through you to all you meet!
   The nighttime nurse who weeps her sorrows
      out
In the privacy of your silent compassion;
   The granddaughter whose same gift of love
Sparkles in her eyes, matching the twinkle in
      your own;
   The doctor whose hands relax
When touching yours, who feels your calm.

I touch,
   I love,
      I heal through you.

And when he had so said, he shewed unto them his hands and his side. Then were the disciples glad, when they saw the Lord.

John 20:20

ALSO

Matthew 25:40
Romans 12:4-5

HANDS

Consider your hands, My dear one. Are they sometimes twisted with pain? Mine were too. See my scars?

Did your hands once caress a downy head or reach for the hand of another in love? Mine do, every day.

Lift your hands in praise of Me! To Me they're beautiful and blessed, for they have done My work.

Consider your hands and rejoice in the tasks they have done for Me down through the years.

I have no hands but yours, and they are all I need.

Amen!

If thou draw out thy soul to the hungry, and satisfy the afflicted soul; then shall thy light rise in obscurity, and thy darkness be as the noonday . . .

Isaiah 58:10

ALSO

Romans 13:10
Matthew 5:16

CHANNEL FOR MY LIGHT

The person talking nonsense down the hall
    Makes so much noise.
I know it's hard for you to love that one,
    My dear, but please do try—for Me.
Once he stood so straight and tall,
    So full of eager joys;
Now brought so low, and never knowing Me . . .
    So love him, with My kind of Charity;
Be My channel—let him see My Light through
    thee.

Yes! Indeed!

That the aged men be sober, grave, temper-
ate, sound in faith, in charity, in patience.
The aged women likewise, that they be in be-
haviour as becometh holiness, not false ac-
cusers, not given to much wine, teachers of
good things. . .

Titus 2:2-3

And he gave some . . . teachers; for the per-
fecting of the saints, for the work of the min-
istry, for the edifying of the body of Christ. . .

Ephesians 4:11-12

BIBLE TEACHER

Gentle hands, warm heart,
    Soft, singing bird,
Always eager to do your part
    To teach My Holy Word.

What's that? All done?
    They've all gone to sleep?
Never mind, My faithful one,
    My Holy Word will keep.

Yes! it will!

Let us even exult in our present sufferings, because we know that suffering trains us to endure, and endurance brings proof that we have stood the test, and this proof is the ground of hope. Such a hope is no mockery, because God's love has flooded our inmost heart through the Holy Spirit he has given us.

Romans 5:3-5 (NEB)

He comforts us in all our troubles, so that we in turn may be able to comfort others in any trouble of theirs and to share with them the consolation we ourselves receive from God. As Christ's cup of suffering overflows, and we suffer with him, so also through Christ our consolation overflows. If distress be our lot, it is the price we pay for your consolation, for your salvation. . .

II Corinthians 1:4-6a (NEB)

ALSO

II Corinthians 5:20

SILENT TEAMWORK

My dear, I know exactly how you feel,
   Lying there, hurting too much to speak,
And anything you'd say has been said before
   And any wisdom that you might reveal
Would not be heard because
   She's much too busy plumping up your
     pillow
Covering over everything with talk.

Don't be impatient with her; she's trying hard;
   She doesn't comprehend the things you feel
Because she is so young!

Let her practice on you, My dear, and smile;
   Through your need and pain, she'll soon
learn
     how to care.
I will guide her ways, and all the while,
   You can lift her up in silent prayer.

To him that overcometh will I give to eat of the tree of life, which is in the midst of the paradise of God.

Revelation 2:7

My grace is all you need; for my power is strongest when you are weak.
II Corinthians 12:9 (Good News for Modern Man)

ALSO
Philippians 1:6

THE OVERCOMER

Ideas flourish in the fertile soil
    of your deep mind,
And toiling upward, find the Light
    where flowering forth,
        they feed My blighted world.

Your flesh has need, but pain
    has merely dared you to succeed.
Thus your weakness is My gain,
    And I see My strength within:
        Ripened fruit from that small seed
    We sowed the day
        You gave your life to Me.

For the same God who said, "Out of darkness let light shine," has caused his light to shine within us, to give the light of revelation—the revelation of the glory of God in the face of Jesus Christ.

II Corinthians 4:6 (NEB)

ALSO

Psalm 139:2, 23
I Corinthians 2:14

THE SILENT ONE

I heard you thinking while they talked
    around you during tea
Of bridge and club and even church,
    but never once of Me.

I know how bored you were, My dear,
    with all the empty chatter
Of love affairs and diets new
    that only make them fatter.

I heard you wish it weren't too late
    to speak to them of Me.
Be still, My love, and know that I
    shone all the while through thee!

Gift of Worship

. . . and he shall rise up at the voice of the bird . . .

Ecclesiastes 12:4

Then God said, Behold, I have given you every plant yielding seed that is on the surface of all the earth . . .

Genesis 1:29 (NAS)

ALSO
John 15:14-15
I Kings 19:12

COMMUNION

I saw you kneeling yesterday
By a sun-drenched daffodil,
And I sat beside you to while away
A summer hour, all still.

I whispered to you and you tipped your head
Like a lightly listening bird,
"Yes, my Lord," you softly said,
And I knew that you had heard.

Make a joyful noise unto God, all ye lands: Sing forth the honour of his name: make his praise glorious.

Psalm 66:1-2

Sing praises to the Lord, which dwelleth in Zion: declare among the people his doings.

Psalm 9:11

Make a joyful noise unto the Lord, all ye lands. Serve the Lord with gladness: come before his presence with singing.

Psalm 100:1-2

MAKE A JOYFUL NOISE

Let's sing today!

Though it may seem only you and I are here, the heavenly angels shall join us and we shall have a choir! Open your mouth and let the praises roll out—the thanksgiving! Lift up adoring hands to Me and you shall hear the bells of joy ringing out!

It's good to make a joyful noise unto the Lord!

And it came to pass, that, while they communed together and reasoned, Jesus himself drew near, and went with them.

Luke 24:15

When thou saidest, Seek ye my face; my heart said unto thee, Thy face, Lord, will I seek.

Psalm 27:8

INTERCESSOR

I was passing by your house last night
    And I looked in the window there,
And I saw you sitting all cheery and bright,
    Caught in a moment's prayer . . .

I felt the pull of your longing need;
    I felt the power drain out,
And I knew that a flower had sprung from the
      seed
    Of a faith that has conquered doubt.

A faith that has grown for fifty years
    Of loving and living and loss,
That has come into bloom, watered with tears
    Shed at the foot of My Cross.

And I knew right away that a healing took place
    Through the Grace of My Father above,
For I looked in your soft and smiling face,
    And I saw My kind of Love.

O clap your hands, all ye people; shout unto God with the voice of triumph.

Psalm 47:1

And Miriam the prophetess, the sister of Aaron, took a timbrel in her hand; and all the women went out after her with timbrels and with dances.

Exodus 15:20

And David danced before the Lord with all his might . . .

II Samuel 6:14

CLAP YOUR HANDS

Clap your hands for you're a saint!
Don't you feel the tingle of excitement?
There's reason: you're triumphant!
Don't you feel alive, alive in Me?
There's reason: I am Life abundant!
Tap your feet: dance with all your
might. There's a reason: I am Light!

Praise to the Lord.

And saith unto them, My soul is exceeding sorrowful unto death: tarry ye here, and watch.

Mark 14:34

Ask, and it shall be given you; seek and ye shall find; knock, and it shall be opened unto you . . .

Matthew 7:7

ALSO

Psalm 23:5
Psalm 103:1-2

TARRY WITH ME

Tarry with Me for My Spirit longs for you! Your prayers are such a blessing to Me, and oh, how I delight to answer them!

Ask and you shall receive blessing overflowing! Lift up your cup and I shall fill it with joy and peace unending.

Do not be afraid to ask because I have so much for you and I desire to give it.

Gift of Renewal

*And be renewed in the spirit of your mind;
And that ye put on the new man, which after
God is created in righteousness and true holi-
ness.*

Ephesians 4:23-24

*Then shall thy light break forth as the mor-
ning, and thine health shall spring forth
speedily . . .*

Isaiah 58:8

ALSO
Genesis 1:31

RENEWAL

Do you know there is renewal in everything I have created? Reach out and touch a flower, a leaf, a snowflake, a raindrop. Are you not aware of Me?

And when it seems these things are gone, behold they come again, restored to life and clothed in beauty—appearing as before, but new.

In just such way I am recreating you. That tired body will be renewed and how tenderly do I fashion you!

. . . ye have put off the old man with his deeds; and have put on the new man, which is renewed in the knowledge after the image of him that created him.

Colossians 3:9-10

And be not conformed to this world: but be ye transformed by the renewing of your mind, that ye may prove what is that good, and acceptable, and perfect, will of God.

Romans 12:2

ALSO
John 3:1-3

TRANSFORMED

Can they possibly imagine
    What it's like to be old?
Always late and always last.
    No longer bold
In anything at all?

Can you recall being young?
    Or was it just too long ago?
Was that another person in the past
    Who laughed so much and moved so fast?

Don't fret. All things are new!
    That child just seems a shadow gone;
For in My Spirit you are young and strong
    And of such infinite worth!

The things that marred are put away,
    And you, who've come to Me
Are new!
    And radiant in new birth!

But they that wait upon the Lord shall renew their strength; they shall mount up with wings as eagles; they shall run and not be weary; and they shall walk and not faint.

Isaiah 40:31

Come, then, stiffen your drooping arms and shaking knees, and keep your steps from wavering. Then the disabled limb will not be put out of joint but regain its former powers.

Hebrews 12:12-13 (NEB)

ALSO

Psalm 103:5
Isaiah 58:8

YOU SHALL BE RENEWED

Dear one, do you sometimes dream of the times past when your feet were steady and sure? And oh, how they loved to dance! This is as nothing compared to what I have prepared for you as you dance before My Father's throne!

With thanksgiving and joy you shall be renewed and will mount up as an eagle!

And I, if I be lifted up from the earth, will draw all men unto me.

John 12:32

. . . For I, the Lord your God, take you by the right hand; I say to you, Do not fear; it is I who help you . . .

Isaiah 41:13-14 (NEB)

ALSO

Ephesians 4:1-2

IF I BE LIFTED UP

I, if I be lifted up
    Will draw all men unto Me;
That is why I took the cup
    And drained it totally.

That you might look up and take My
      Hand
    And let Me set you free,
That you might finally understand
    What it is to live with Me.

And the pain of it all was worth it to see
    The perfection of My Grace
That flows from you when you think of
      Me
    And lights up your loving face.

My son, do not think lightly of the Lord's discipline, nor lose heart when he corrects you; for the Lord disciplines those whom he loves; he lays the rod on every son whom he acknowledges.

Hebrews 12:5b-6 (NEB)

And for their sakes I sanctify myself, that they also might be sanctified through the truth.

John 17:19

ALSO

Psalm 147:3
Revelation 4:4, 21:5

YOU ARE A NEW CREATION

Many trials you have had in this life, but the Father chasteneth those whom He loves the most. He binds up your wounds and His love flows over the scars, and they are no more.

You are a new creation, pure and spotless, sanctified. His robes of righteousness are upon you and you are beautiful to behold.

David and all Israel danced for joy before God without restraint to the sound of singing, of harps and lutes, of tambourines, and cymbals and trumpets.

I Chronicles 13:8 (NEB)

ALSO

Psalm 95
Romans 8:2

Gift of Immortality

In my Father's house are many mansions: if it were not so, I would have told you. I go to prepare a place for you. And if I go and prepare a place for you, I will come again, and receive you unto myself; that where I am, there ye may be also. And whither I go ye know, and the way ye know.

John 14:2-4

And the city had no need of the sun, neither of the moon, to shine in it: for the glory of God did lighten it, and the Lamb is the light thereof.

Revelation 21:23

MY FATHER'S HOUSE

Today you are thinking of your loved ones who have gone ahead and are in My Father's house. With what joy and anticipation they are waiting to greet you when you have finished your time here in your earthly home! With outstretched arms they will meet you. We will take you through the valley to the place prepared for you—to the Everlasting Light, beyond anything you have dreamed of!

I am the resurrection, and the life: he that believeth in me, though he were dead, yet shall he live: And whosoever liveth and believeth in me shall never die. Believest thou this?

John 11:25-26

For we know that if our earthly house of this tabernacle were dissolved, we have a building of God, an house not made with hands, eternal in the heavens.

II Corinthians 5:1

ALSO
John 14:5-6

THE WAY

Did you hear Me calling in the wind
    a couple of nights ago?
Did you hear Me asking, "Where've you been?
    and say, "I love you so"?

Did you hear Me whisper in your ear
    how beautiful it will be?
That there is nothing at all to fear
    when it's time to come to Me?

It's lovely here; the weather's fine!
    There's plenty for you to do!
Your friends said to tell you, "It's divine."
    With joy they're waiting for you.

But please don't fret; there's no big rush;
    I simply want to say
That in the beauty and the hush
    of prayer, I'll show the way.

But some man will say, How are the dead raised up? and with what body do they come? . . . But God giveth it a body as it hath pleased him, and to every seed his own body. . . . So also is the resurrection of the dead. It is sown in corruption; it is raised in incorruption: It is sown in dishonour; it is raised in glory: it is sown in weakness; it is raised in power: It is sown a natural body; it is raised a spiritual body. . . . Behold, I show you a mystery; We shall not all sleep, but we shall all be changed. In a moment, in the twinkling of an eye at the last trump: for the trumpet shall sound, and the dead shall be raised incorruptible, and we shall be changed. . . . So when this corruptible shall have put on incorruption, and this mortal shall have put on immortality, then shall be brought to pass the saying that is written, Death is swallowed up in victory. O death, where is thy sting? O grave, where is thy victory?

I Corinthians 15:35, 38, 42-44a, 51-52, 54-55

THE LAST GIFT

A time shall come
    When prison walls will fall:
Your eager spirit caged so long
    Shall leap out into Light!
And on that day
    I'll wipe away all tears.

Pain of age can never more destroy
    Your peace; no endless years,
No loneliness, no fears
    Shall mar your joy.

No more your flesh
    Shall rage against infirmity.
This earthly frame shall fall,
    And then I'll fashion one for you,
Incorruptible and new,
    For all eternity!

The drawings which appear on the division pages were done by Lois Cowley of Denver, Colorado. Her work is represented in collections throughout the world. Whether she is painting a landscape, an oil portrait of a celebrity or child, sculpting in bronze or sketching animals and flowers, her work reflects a sensitive respect for beauty and discipline. To her, creating is a spiritual experience and comes from a God-given talent.